HAPPY READING!.

K. W. Wilson

It All Starts With YOU!

K.W. Wilson

Illustrated by Josh Flanigan

HayMarBooks, LLC
Copyrighted Material
It All Starts With You

For information about this title or to order other books
and/or electronic media, contact the publisher:

HayMarBooks, LLC
Jacksonville, FL 32223

www.haymarbooks.com
dianeharper@haymarbooks.com

Library of Congress Control Number:
2013905109

ISBN: 978-0-9848736-4-7 Hardcover

Cover and Interior Design: 1106 Design
Cover and Interior Illustrations: Josh Flanigan

Printed in the United States of America

Acknowledgements

This book is dedicated to Mary Lou Blackley, for her lifelong love and passion to better the lives of all the children she could. Her work lives on.

I would like to thank all my family for being very supportive of this venture in my life; specifically Brian and Denise Blackley, my sisters Brianne Blackley and Shanley Sifain, and brother-in-law Andrew Sifain for their endless (and often biased) opinions to the good and bad ideas along the way. And a very special thanks to my nephew Jaemison Clark, just because he's cool.

Thanks go out to all my friends who supported me along the way, from their input for the manuscript and yeah-you-can-do-this attitude, all the way to trips and "business meetings," to seek out illustrators for this project. To Daniel Mault, Nicole Stymus, AnnaLynn Williams and others too numerous to name; thank you for your support.

Last but not least, it could not have been done without Diane Harper, also known as D.W. Harper, and her independent publishing company HayMarBooks, LLC. The endless support, advice, answers, and push to succeed really paid off.

Little Mickey was nervous about his first day at school.
He wanted all the kids to think he was cool.

But he was a little too short, his hair a little too red.
He was a little too skinny and looked a little underfed.

As he walked down the hall, the first day of the year,
he wasn't very happy, no excitement, no cheer.

Some kids were mean, some made him sad,
some made him nervous, some made him mad.

He had to do something to show he wasn't a snore.
He saw Lizzie coming, so he pushed her to the floor.

The reason he did that, he didn't know why,
the reason he did that, but it made Lizzie cry.

Why are we mean? What can we do?
We can make things better, and it can start with you!

Lizzie had a problem.
When she tried to say a word,
what was on her mind
sometimes came out slurred.

12

Some day she'd outgrow it. It was only a matter of time.
Before she'd even know it, her speech would be just fine. 13

But as Lizzie walked to lunch, she felt hurt and sad.
Why would Mickey shove her? What made him so mad?

Some kids were mean, some made her sad,
some made her nervous, some made her mad.

15

When Lizzie spotted Charlie, she wasn't very nice.
"Hey there, Big Charlie, did you eat lunch twice?"

The reason she did that, she didn't know why,
the reason she did that, but it made Charlie cry.

Why are we mean? What can we do?
We can make things better, and it can start with you!

Nikki was smart. She worked hard for her grades. But some students were jealous that she got all A's.

Nikki was quiet, and Charlie was loud.
He wanted good grades so his parents were proud.

That day in the classroom, as Nikki did math,
Charlie walked over and stood in her path.

Some kids were mean, some made him sad,
some made him nervous, some made him mad.

"Your eyes are so small! You have teeth like a bunny!
I wouldn't smile anymore, it makes you look funny."

23

The reason he did that, he didn't know why,
the reason he did that, but it made Nikki cry.

Why are we mean? What can we do?
We can make things better, and it can start with you!

Nikki saw Mickey waiting for the bus.
She knew how to hurt him, so she started a fuss.

26

"**Y**ou have silly red hair! I think it's funny you're small!
I bet you wish you looked different! I bet you wish you were tall!" 27

Now all four kids shared the same pain.
They all hurt each other, but did anyone gain?

They wanted to fix it and knew that they could.
The next day at school was the first day they would!

29

Mickey wasn't mean, so Lizzie wasn't sad,
so Charlie wasn't nervous, so Nikki wasn't mad.

Let's all get along and make a new friend!
Be nice to each other! Start a new trend!

Being different is okay! Being yourself is, too.
Every person is special, just like you.

We don't have to be mean! You know it's true!
Let's make things better! It all starts with you!

About the Author

K.W. Wilson was born and raised in Lockport, NY. He is the youngest of three children. While in elementary school under the guidance of the C.L.A.S.S. Program, he penned his first memorable story. It was a remastered tale of Hansel and Gretel from the witch's perspective. That project had a profound impact on him, inspiring him to dream of publishing a book.

He is a 2004 graduate of Lockport Senior High School and received a Bachelor of Science in Accounting and Master of Business Administration in Forensic Accounting from Canisius College. K.W. Wilson currently resides in Buffalo, NY, working as a Controller for a private company.

The goal for *It All Starts With You* is to raise awareness for the ever-increasing problem of bullying, while also spreading a message of positivity and change. Too many kids are affected by bullying on a daily basis. If parents, teachers and our society can help young minds understand the power of one person's actions, we can begin to make the world a nicer, happier place.

About the Illustrator

Josh Flanigan has literally been drawing since he could pick up a pencil. As a teenager and young adult a sketchbook was his constant companion. While working at restaurants, he would draw charicatures of his co-workers on the back side of the placemats. A Western New York native, Josh studied illustration at Bryant & Stratton College and the Art Institute of Pittsburgh. He has worked as a graphic designer and illustrator since 1998 and currently works at *Buffalo Spree* magazine and is a contributor on Shutterstock.com. He is madly in love with his wife of 14 years and appreciates her support. He has three school-age children and was excited about spreading the word against bullying through his work on this book. He believes in the golden rule and always tries to treat others as he would like to be treated.

CPSIA information can be obtained
at www.ICGtesting.com
Printed in the USA
LVIC061102070613
337412LV00001B